The Chick That Wouldn't Hatch

Claire Daniel

Illustrated by Lisa Campbell Ernst

Green Light Readers
Harcourt, Inc.
Orlando   Austin   New York   San Diego   Toronto   London

There were six eggs in Hen's nest.
Chip! Chip! Chip! Chip! Chip!
Out popped five chicks.

"My family!" cried Hen.
One egg didn't hatch. It rolled out
of the nest.

Pig couldn't catch it, so he ran, too.
The egg kept going.

It rolled over and over, past the pond.
"Stop that egg!" called Hen and Pig.

Duck couldn't catch it, so she ran, too.
The egg kept going.

It rolled over again and again, past the
tomato patch.
"Stop that egg!" called Hen and Pig and Duck.

Horse couldn't catch it, so he ran, too.
The egg skipped over a ditch.

"Stop! Stop!" cried Hen.
It hopped over a fox.

The egg rolled into the shed and hit the wall. *CRACK!* The chick that wouldn't hatch had hatched!

"My baby!" Hen cried.
"Mom!" said the chick. "What a ride I had!"
"Yes," said Hen, "and what a run we had!"

Hatching an Egg

You can make the chick that wouldn't hatch.

WHAT YOU'LL NEED

- paper
- crayons or markers
- scissors
- tape

1. Cut out two egg shapes.

2. Draw a chick on one egg.

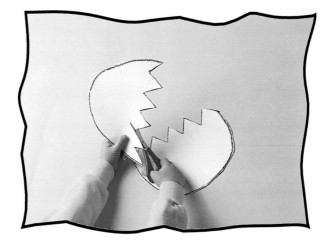

3. Cut the other egg in half.

4. Tape one half at the top
and the other half at
the bottom.

Use your hatching egg to
tell a friend about

the chick that wouldn't hatch!

Meet the Illustrator

While Lisa Campbell Ernst was drawing the pictures for *The Chick That Wouldn't Hatch*, she took her daughter to the zoo. Her daughter loved a horse she saw there named Lance. So Lisa Campbell Ernst painted the horse in this book to look just like Lance. She hopes that you draw the things you see around you, too!

Lisa Campbell Ernst

Requests for permission to make copies of any part of the work should be mailed
to the following address: Permissions Department, Harcourt, Inc.,
6277 Sea Harbor Drive, Orlando, Florida 32887-6777.

www.HarcourtBooks.com

First Green Light Readers edition 1999
Green Light Readers is a trademark of Harcourt, Inc., registered in the United States
of America and/or other jurisdictions.

The Library of Congress has cataloged an earlier edition as follows:
Daniel, Claire.
The chick that wouldn't hatch/written by Claire Daniel;
illustrated by Lisa Campbell Ernst.
p. cm.
"Green Light Readers."
Summary: Before she hatches from her egg, a baby chick takes quite a trip
around the farm—with her mother and other animals in pursuit.
[1. Eggs—Fiction. 2. Chicken—Fiction.] I. Ernst, Lisa Campbell, ill.
II. Title. III. Series.
PZ7.D216Ch 1999
[E]—dc21 98-55235
ISBN 0-15-204871-5
ISBN 0-15-204831-6 (pb)

A C E G H F D B
A C E G H F D B (pb)

Ages 5–7
Grade: 1
Guided Reading Level: F–G
Reading Recovery Level: 13–14

Green Light Readers
For the reader who's ready to GO!

"A must-have for any family with a beginning reader."—*Boston Sunday Herald*

"You can't go wrong with adding several copies of these terrific books to your beginning-to-read collection."—*School Library Journal*

"A winner for the beginner."—*Booklist*

Five Tips to Help Your Child Become a Great Reader

1. Get involved. Reading aloud to and with your child is just as important as encouraging your child to read independently.

2. Be curious. Ask questions about what your child is reading.

3. Make reading fun. Allow your child to pick books on subjects that interest her or him.

4. Words are everywhere—not just in books. Practice reading signs, packages, and cereal boxes with your child.

5. Set a good example. Make sure your child sees YOU reading.

Why Green Light Readers Is the Best Series for Your New Reader

● Created exclusively for beginning readers by some of the biggest and brightest names in children's books

● Reinforces the reading skills your child is learning in school

● Encourages children to read—and finish—books by themselves

● Offers extra enrichment through fun, age-appropriate activities unique to each story

● Incorporates characteristics of the Reading Recovery program used by educators

● Developed with Harcourt School Publishers and credentialed educational consultants

Daniel's Mystery Egg
Alma Flor Ada/G. Brian Karas

Animals on the Go
Jessica Brett/Richard Cowdrey

Marco's Run
Wesley Cartier/Reynold Ruffins

Digger Pig and the Turnip
Caron Lee Cohen/Christopher Denise

Tumbleweed Stew
Susan Stevens Crummel/Janet Stevens

The Chick That Wouldn't Hatch
Claire Daniel/Lisa Campbell Ernst

Splash!
Ariane Dewey/Jose Aruego

Get That Pest!
Erin Douglas/Wong Herbert Yee

Why the Frog Has Big Eyes
Betsy Franco/Joung Un Kim

I Wonder
Tana Hoban

A Bed Full of Cats
Holly Keller

The Fox and the Stork
Gerald McDermott

Boots for Beth
Alex Moran/Lisa Campbell Ernst

Catch Me If You Can!
Bernard Most

The Very Boastful Kangaroo
Bernard Most

Farmers Market
Carmen Parks/Edward Martinez

Shoe Town
Janet Stevens/Susan Stevens Crummel

The Enormous Turnip
Alexei Tolstoy/Scott Goto

Where Do Frogs Come From?
Alex Vern

The Purple Snerd
Rozanne Lanczak Williams/
Mary GrandPré

Look for more Green Light Readers wherever books are sold!